Rapunzel

Other brilliant stories to collect:

Rapunzel

Retold by
Jacqueline Wilson

Illustrated by
Nick Sharratt

SCHOLASTIC
Home of the Story

Scholastic Children's Books,
Commonwealth House, 1–19 New Oxford Street,
London WC1A 1NU, UK
a division of Scholastic Ltd
London ~ New York ~ Toronto ~ Sydney ~ Auckland
Mexico City ~ New Delhi ~ Hong Kong

First published by Scholastic Ltd, 1998

Text copyright © Jacqueline Wilson, 1998
Illustrations copyright © Nick Sharratt, 1998

ISBN 0 590 11363 1

Printed and bound by Mackays of Chatham

2 4 6 8 10 9 7 5 3 1

The right of Jacqueline Wilson and Nick Sharratt to be identified
as the author and illustrator respectively of this work has been
asserted by them in accordance with the
Copyright, Designs and Patents Act, 1988.

There was once a husband and wife who longed for a child. The man made a cradle out of oak and carved buttercups and daisies round the side. The woman sewed many silk outfits and embroidered flocks of lovebirds and butterflies on every single baby garment.

The years went by. The cradle gathered dust in a corner because the woman couldn't bear to go near it. The baby clothes stayed shut in a drawer, the bright birds and butterflies trapped in the dark.

The husband hoped his wife might accept her lot as she grew older but if anything her longing grew worse. Sometimes he saw her fold her arms and rock them as if she were holding an invisible baby. He couldn't stand seeing her aching so badly.

The couple lived in a cottage at the edge of the village. The very last house was a forbidding dark dwelling with dragons painted on the door and a glowering griffin weathervane on the roof. The garden was surrounded by a high wall but the husband and wife could peep down into it when they were upstairs in their cottage.

It was no ordinary garden of cornflowers and cabbages. They recognized

some of the plants, lavender, mint, camomile, foxglove . . . but there were many strange herbs they'd never seen before.

They rarely spied their neighbour, a wild-looking old woman with tangled grey hair and stark black clothing. She sold herbal remedies and acted as a midwife — but most of the villagers shunned her, whispering that she was a witch. One stupid small boy dared torment her, climbing her wall and pulling up some of her plants. That night he had a fit, fell into a trance, and never walked or talked again.

The husband and wife steered well clear of their neighbour – but the husband couldn't help wondering if she might have some magic potion that could help them have a child. She was a midwife, after all. She might know some special secrets.

One morning the wife discovered a strand of grey in her fair hair. She started weeping because she knew she

was almost too old to have a baby now. The sound of her sobs spurred the husband on.

He walked out of the cottage, down the garden path, out of his wooden gate – and through the sharply spiked iron arch belonging to his neighbour. He stood still in the strange garden, staring all around him. The cobbled path seemed to tilt first one way, then the other, making him dizzy. He forced himself towards the house, plants brushing against his ankles with their bristly leaves, creepers coiling round his calves as if they had a

life of their own.

It took him all his courage to seize the leering lion's head knocker. It was horribly hot to the touch so that he only dared one timid rap before snatching his hand away. The door opened almost immediately. The bent old woman stood before him, squinting up at him from behind her grey hanks of hair.

"I'm so sorry to disturb you, Madam," the husband said. "It's just that I couldn't help wondering. . . You seem so learned in matters of magic. . ." His voice tailed away.

The old woman waited, rubbing her dry old hands together so that they made a rasping noise.

"It's my wife," the husband continued desperately. "She's always longed for a child and now I'm so scared this longing is driving her demented. Is there any way at all you can help? Some pill, some potion, some secret spell? I'm not a rich man but I'd be willing to give you all my savings – a purse of gold – if you will help us."

The old woman's mouth tightened until her dry lips disappeared.

"I have always longed for a

daughter myself," she said, her old eyes watering.

The husband stared at her in astonishment, amazed that a weird old witch woman could want a child.

"Do not look so surprised," she said bitterly. She sniffed and composed herself. "However, you have been courteous. I do know a few secret tricks that might work." She whispered in his ear. "And make your wife a special rapunzel salad tonight."

"Rapunzel?" said the husband.

"You might call it rampion. It's a salad delicacy."

"We haven't got any rampion in our vegetable garden. Would lettuce do instead?" said the husband.

"It won't do at all," said the old woman. "Here, I have a special rampion patch myself. I will pick you a bunch. But I can only spare you a little."

"It's very kind of you to spare me any," said the husband gratefully. "What do I owe you?" He rather hoped she wasn't going to charge him too many pieces of gold for a couple of tips and a bunch of green leaves.

"You don't owe me anything, neighbour. But do not come back and

trouble me again," said the old
woman, and she shut her door.

The husband went back to his wife
and told her he'd consulted with the
old woman. She was impressed by his
courage, but did not think the witch's
tricks would work – though she ate all
her rampion salad supper with great
relish.

Weeks passed. The husband and

wife dared start hoping. Months passed. The wife's gown grew tight around her waist. She clasped her rounded stomach, her face soft with joy.

"I am going to have a baby!" she said.

The husband put his arms around his dear wife and they both wept with happiness.

The wife was not very well during the months she carried her child. She had to rest in her bed many days and she was often sick.

"You must eat something, my love. You have to nourish our baby as well as yourself," said the husband.

"I can't fancy any food at all — except that strange rampion," said the wife. "Oh, I so long for that sweet delicious fresh tangy taste. Can't you ask the old witch for some more?"

"She said she could only spare me a little. And she warned me not to trouble her again." The husband

hesitated. "But I could try telling her just how much it would mean to you."

So he went round to the old woman. She glared at him when she opened her door. He told her his wife was now with child and begged for another bunch of rampion.

"I told you, I cannot spare you any more."

"She craves the taste so."

"Then she must go on craving," said the old woman sharply. "I'm warning you! You will bitterly regret it if you disturb me again."

The wife wept when told of the old

woman's refusal. She sat up in bed all day and half the night, looking down into the garden where she could see the green rampion patch. Her stomach was still round, but her face grew pale and pinched and the flesh fell away from her arms and legs. The husband was tormented with this new worry, scared his wife would not survive her pregnancy.

He knew there was no point begging the old woman once more. He decided to take matters into his own hands. He knew what he had to do.

He waited until long past mid-

night when the moon was hidden by clouds. Then he crept out of his house in his stockinged feet. The iron arch was locked but he climbed up and over it, though hidden spikes tore great grooves in his hands. He sucked his bloody fingers and stumbled up and down the cobbled path, trying to locate the rampion patch. A huge creeper wound itself right round his neck like a cobra and gave him such a shock he fell headlong. He lay stunned for a moment — and then realized he had fallen right into the rampion patch.

He plucked as many leaves as he could, scrambled to his feet, and was just stumbling back to the gate when he heard the front door open.

The moon came out, a huge pearly full moon that cast an eerie silver glow upon the garden. The old woman stood right in front of him, her eyes glittering, her face contorted, her mouth open. Her few teeth were filed into points. She looked as if she could tear out his throat with one bite.

"How dare you steal from me!" she shrieked.

"Oh please, have mercy! I know I shouldn't have tried — but my wife is so ill and craves your rampion so very badly, you have no idea."

"Yes, I have no idea," said the old woman, hugging her bent old body tight with her crooked hands.

"Can't you take pity on us?" the husband begged. "If my wife cannot eat your rampion she will surely die."

The old woman said nothing for a long, long while. A little trickle of saliva slid from between her pointed teeth and dribbled down her chin. Her eyes gleamed like a wild cat's. The

husband wondered whether to try to make a run for it but his sodden feet seemed planted in her garden and he could scarcely move a muscle. He realized he was under a terrible enchantment.

"Please, I beg you, have mercy!" he gasped. "I will do anything, give you anything, if you will let me go back to my wife."

"Anything at all?" said the old woman.

"Anything at all," the husband repeated desperately. "I swear it."

"Then your wife shall have all the rampion she can eat," said the old

woman, stooping down and gathering great fistfuls of it. She thrust them at the husband, who found he could wrench his feet free again. "But, in return. . ."

He waited, heart thudding.

The old woman raised her head and pointed a shaking finger.

"In return. . . If your wife has a daughter you must give the child to me."

The husband gasped and implored but the old woman turned her back on him and shut herself into her dark house.

He took the rampion back to his ailing wife. She seized it joyously, eating it straight from his hand, not even bothering to wash the earth away.

"Thank the Lord the old witch didn't catch you!" she said.

The husband didn't dare tell her what had happened. He could not stand to worry her so. Besides, they might well have a son.

He consulted all the other old

women in the village to see if they had any way of divining the sex of the unborn child. His wife laughed as they dandled rings on ribbons above her swollen stomach.

"I don't care whether our baby is a boy or a girl," she said.

"I care," said the husband. He shut his eyes as if he were praying. "It has to be a boy."

"It will be a boy," cried the old women as the ring swung backwards and forwards.

"A baby boy," said the wife, and she sounded pleased.

She looked so much better, a pink flush to her cheek. She bloomed throughout the rest of her pregnancy like a sweet round peach. The husband grew thin and pale with dread.

"It has to be a boy," he muttered, his hands on the wife's stomach.

He could feel the baby kicking within.

"My son," he whispered.

"Our son," said the wife.

But it wasn't a son. The wife had an easy labour and gave birth to a beautiful blonde daughter.

"A girl!" said the husband, and burst into tears.

"Our daughter," said the wife.

"My daughter," said the old witch-woman, suddenly appearing in the room as if she had leapt through the window. She seized hold of the newborn child, still pink and naked, and held her tight against her sunken chest.

"No!" screamed the wife, trying to get out of bed, but stuck fast.

"No!" shouted the husband, reaching out his arms, but able to grasp nothing.

"Yes," said the old woman, wrapping the baby in a blanket and cradling her. "She is my daughter now and I name her Rapunzel." She looked over at the anguished wife. "Do not worry, I will be a loving mother to the child."

"My child," the wife gasped.

"Mine now," said the old woman. "But perhaps fate will still be kind to you and grant you another. Eat my rampion whenever you wish. I am

going to be far, far away."

And with that she wrapped her cloak around herself and the child . . . and vanished.

The old woman set up home in another village the other end of the country. She laid out another elaborate herb garden and sewed it with many seeds – but no rampion. She looked after Rapunzel with loving care, singing to

the child at night, telling her magical stories, teaching her the names of all the herbs and how to turn them into potions and remedies. She did not send Rapunzel to the village school when she was five. She taught the child to read and write herself.

The old woman and Rapunzel kept very much to themselves, but as the girl grew older children came calling every day, desperate to see and talk and play with the strange little girl with such old-fashioned sweet manners and such amazing hair. Rapunzel was a bonnie baby and a pretty little

girl but by the time she got to eleven it was obvious she was growing into a stunning beauty. She had a lovely face and a lithe form but the most wondrous thing about her was her hair. It was thick and blonde with a natural wave. The old woman washed it with special herbal shampoo and brushed it a hundred strokes each night with an ivory-backed bristle brush. Rapunzel's hair grew long and strong and shining. It was down past her shoulders by the time she was two, curling at her waist by five, gently brushing the backs of her knees at eight, and now at eleven

Rapunzel's hair swept the floor like a golden train.

Of course this was scarcely practical, so during the day the old woman braided it, her shaking fingers surprisingly nimble as she plaited each heavy silken strand, and then she looped the braids up so that Rapunzel had her own golden halo of hair. It was so heavy on her head that it was always a great relief to untie it all at bedtime. The old woman would sometimes plunge her hands into its warmth or delicately finger one little curl. Once she felt her own sparse

grey straggles and sighed.

"I expect you had long golden hair when you were little, Mother," said Rapunzel. "But anyway, I think grey hair is very distinguished."

"You are a sweet child, daughter," said the old woman. "You do love me, don't you, Rapunzel?"

"More than anyone in the world, Mother," said Rapunzel.

"And you never feel you'd be happier living anywhere else?"

"I only ever want to live with you," said Rapunzel.

There was a knock on the door at

that moment. Half a dozen ragged boys from the village had come to call on Rapunzel. The old woman sent them away curtly. A few days later a young nobleman from a nearby castle came to see this girl with the wondrous hair for himself. The old woman sent him away with equal abruptness. The next day three more young men came calling.

"Do we have to send them all away, Mother?" said Rapunzel. "It might be pleasant to have company from time to time."

"We are company. We don't need

anyone else," said the old woman gruffly.

The callers became such a problem as Rapunzel's hair grew to ever more fabulous golden lengths that the old woman became desperate. She worked her magical powers to the ultimate and then woke Rapunzel very early on her twelfth birthday and told her she had an astonishing present for her. She

said it was hidden deep in the forest.

"Why did you hide it away there, Mother?" asked Rapunzel.

"So that no one else will see it. It's our very own special secret," said the old woman, taking Rapunzel by the hand.

They walked far into the dark forest. Rapunzel couldn't help being a little frightened, especially when an animal snarled in the distance or a bird suddenly soared in the air, almost entangling itself in Rapunzel's abundant tresses.

"Are we nearly there, Mother?"

"Very nearly, my dear," said the old woman.

She held Rapunzel's hand very tightly indeed. The trees suddenly thinned and they stepped into a sunlit round clearing edged by tall protective oaks. Skylarks spiralled high in the air above, squirrels scampered in the grass below. At the very centre of the clearing was a shining golden tower.

Rapunzel stood still, dazzled.

"What is this beautiful tower, Mother?"

"It's a new home, daughter dearest," said the old woman.

"Our new home?" said Rapunzel.

"Your new home, Rapunzel," said the old woman.

She pointed to the tower. It shone so strongly in the sunlight that Rapunzel had to hide her eyes. The light seared her very eyelids and she had to crouch down, her arms over her head. She seemed to be whirled around, up and up and up . . . and then suddenly she found herself curled on the floor. She wasn't lying on the grass in the sunlight. She was crouching on dark red carpet.

Rapunzel lifted her head and stared all around her. She was in a round red chamber, a beautiful room with velvet couches and crimson tapestries and ruby glass lamps. There was a table set with all her favourite dishes, a chest of beautiful dresses all colours of the rainbow, a shelf of all her special childhood toys. There was a bed with a deep rose coverlet and a pink satin pillow, a dressing table set with her

own ivory-backed hairbrush.

"My home?" Rapunzel whispered. And then she shouted, "Mother? Mother, where are you? *Mother!*"

"Come to the window, Rapunzel," the old woman called.

Rapunzel picked herself up and ran to the one high-up window in the room. She peered down . . . and there was the old woman far below.

"Mother! Why have you shut me up in the tower alone?" Rapunzel screamed.

"I have to keep you safe, my darling," the old woman said. "Don't be

afraid. You will be so happy in your special tower. I will come and visit you every single day. I will bring you fresh food and brush your beautiful hair and tell you stories and sing you to sleep."

"But how will you get in? There's no door to the chamber, no way into the tower," said Rapunzel.

"It will be simple, my child. I shall call up to you, 'Rapunzel, Rapunzel, let down your long hair,' and you will let down your wondrous long hair braided into a rope. It will reach nearly to the ground. I will climb up and be

with you," said the old woman.
"That's how I will get in."

"But . . . how will I get out?" said
Rapunzel.

The old woman did not answer.
Rapunzel realized she was trapped.

She spent weeks trying to work out a
way to escape. If she jumped straight
out of the window she would be
dashed to death. She stared at the

tiny squirrels far down below. She couldn't climb down because the golden bricks were smooth as glass. She looked up at the skylarks above and wished she had wings.

She examined every inch of her deep red room, pulling up the carpet, wrenching the heavy cupboard from the wall, but she could not find a crack or a chink anywhere. There was no sign of a way out. She was trapped, trapped, trapped.

Every day the old woman would come and call, "Rapunzel, Rapunzel, let down your long hair."

Rapunzel would throw down her massive braid and the old woman would haul herself up and up and up, through the window and into Rapunzel's chamber. She brought Rapunzel a new present every day — another beautiful gown, a phial of perfume, a story book, a singing bird in a cage. Sometimes Rapunzel was grateful and hugged the old woman and they had happy times together. Sometimes Rapunzel was restless and resentful.

"I don't want your presents. I don't want you. Just let me out!" she

screamed, and she tore her gown and spilt the perfume and threw the book out of the window and let the bird out of its cage to fly free.

But after a while Rapunzel stopped rebelling. She went about her daily tasks in a dream. She behaved in a kindly way to the old woman, but with no feeling. Every evening by herself she watched the sun set and sang a sad sweet lament as the blue sky became as red as her own room.

One evening a prince lost his way as he rode through the forest. His horse stumbled into the clearing. The prince was surprised by the golden tower – and when he heard the sweet song the hair stood up on the back of his neck. He got down from his horse and went round and round the tower, looking for the way in. The song went on and on up above, and he felt desperate to see the singer. But there was

no way in and he eventually gave up and rode away.

He came back to the clearing every evening, utterly enchanted by the sweetness and sadness of the song, nearly driven demented by his desire. He came earlier and earlier. One day he came so early he saw the old woman stumbling along towards the tower. He hid behind one of the oaks and watched her crane her neck and call up, "Rapunzel, Rapunzel, let down your long hair."

He held his breath as a great golden rope of hair tumbled down from the

high window. He watched as the old woman clambered upwards, up and up and up – and in the window. The hair was withdrawn. He waited and watched a long time. Eventually the golden rope was thrown out and the old woman wobbled her way down and down its fabulous length until her old pointed boots touched the grass. He let her hobble off out of sight.

He waited, his heart racing, his fists clenched. Then he approached the foot of the tower, craned his neck, and called up in a cracked, old-woman voice, "Rapunzel, Rapunzel, let down

your long hair."

The amazingly long strong braid of hair swung down out of the window. The prince seized it eagerly, marvelling at its warm silkiness, and started climbing up and up and up . . . and in at the window.

Rapunzel screamed as he jumped into the midst of her chamber. She tried to run, but she'd wound her hair round a hook at the window to relieve the strain on her scalp and she was caught fast.

"Allow me," said the Prince, and he deftly unhooked her and helped her

haul her hair back up into the room.

Rapunzel wrapped her plait around herself in her anxiety.

"I thought you were Mother returning. Where is she? You haven't harmed her?"

"Of course not, Madam."

"Who are you? You're not one of the boys from the village?"

The Prince stood up straight, displaying his courtly clothes.

"I am a Prince," he informed her. "And you must be an enchanted Princess, shut up in this golden tower."

"I'm not a Princess. I'm only Rapunzel," she said, giggling.

"You're a Princess to me," said the Prince, and he took her hand and kissed it.

He stayed very late that night. He came the next day, after the old woman had paid her visit. He stayed even later. He came every evening at sunset, courting his beautiful

Rapunzel — and now he did not leave until sunrise. He loved Rapunzel with all his heart and soul and she loved him too, deeply and passionately.

"How can I carry you away, my darling Rapunzel? I want to take you to my Palace and make you my real Princess," said the Prince, stroking the long shimmering waterfall of her hair. "You're so beautiful. Your hair is so strong and yet it's so silky too."

Rapunzel started. "Skeins of silk!" she said. "That's it. Bring me a skein of silk every time you visit me, dearest Prince. I will braid them tight and

strong so that they make a ladder. When the ladder is long enough I will tie it to the window hook and climb down from the tower into your arms."

It seemed a splendid plan. The Prince did as she suggested and brought a skein of silk every day. Rapunzel spent hours every day constructing the silken ladder. It was good to have something to do with her time. Since the Prince started visiting her she had grown bored with all her old childish games. She could not even amuse herself dressing up in all her rainbow gowns because many of them

did not fit her any more. Even the loosest purple gown was growing tighter and tighter at the waist.

The old woman seemed to be growing smaller and frailer as Rapunzel grew bigger and more bonnie. She had difficulty clambering up the rope of Rapunzel's hair. Rapunzel had to reach out when she got to the window to haul her in.

One morning the effort was so great that the taut seams on her purple gown couldn't take the strain any more. As she pulled the old woman into her chamber Rapunzel's dress tore almost in two and slithered about her thickening waist. The old woman stared at her soft new curves and gave a great howl of realization.

"You are going to have a child!" she gasped.

Rapunzel was very frightened — and yet in the midst of her fear and anxiety a deep happiness made her blush.

"I am going to have the Prince's

baby!" she said. "Oh, how wonder-ful!"

"You wicked deceitful ungrateful girl! You are no longer my daughter," screamed the old woman.

She seized a pair of sharp scissors and cut her way straight through Rapunzel's wonderful plait, sawing it right off at the nape of her neck. Then she took the girl and shook her hard until the red chamber whirled all around her and Rapunzel's eyes rolled up and she fell down down down into darkness. . .

When she awoke she was alone in a

barren desert. She put her poor shorn head on her knees and wept.

The old woman stayed hidden in Rapunzel's tower. Towards sunset the Prince came eagerly to meet up with his love.

"Rapunzel, Rapunzel, let down your long hair," he called.

The witch took Rapunzel's cut-off braid, secured one end to the window

hook and let the golden plait slither down to the ground. The prince climbed up and up and up, and put one leg over the window ledge – and then stopped dead, staring at the old woman in front of him, her face contorted with rage.

"Where is Rapunzel?" he gasped.

"She is gone – and you will never see her again," the old woman screamed.

She pushed the Prince hard so that he fell back out of the window, down and down and down. Thorn bushes suddenly sprouted out of the green

grass. The Prince landed in these thorns and was almost torn to pieces. Two big thorns pierced his eyes so that he could no longer see.

He stumbled off in this new dark world, calling for Rapunzel.

He felt his way right through the forest and journeyed to and fro across the land, blindly searching for his lost love. A year went by, and then another. Time had no meaning for the Prince. He knew he had to search for Rapunzel to the end of his days.

But then, one evening when there was a beautiful blood-red sunset

(though of course he couldn't see it) the Prince heard the sweetest saddest singing. It was very soft and far away – but unmistakable.

"Rapunzel!" he said, and he started running, stumbling and tapping his stick before him frantically.

Rapunzel stopped singing for an instant, hearing his dear voice calling her name.

"My Prince?" she said, and she ran out of the makeshift hovel that was now her home.

She saw a blind man in rags staggering towards her – but knew at

once who he was.

"My Prince!" she cried, tears of joy rolling down her cheeks.

"Rapunzel!" cried the Prince. He threw away his stick and held out his arms.

Rapunzel ran right into his embrace. Her tears fell on his wounded eyes, washing out the deeply-embedded thorns. The Prince could see again. He saw his own beloved Rapunzel, her hair now growing way past her shoulders. He also saw the rosy-cheeked fair twins tumbling outdoors to meet their father for

the first time.

The Prince took his family back to his Kingdom where they lived happily ever after.

The distraught old witch-woman wandered the world but ended up back in her original old cottage with dragons on the door and the griffin weathervane on the roof. Rapunzel's parents had moved away, but the

villagers said the wife had given birth to a fine son a year after she lost her daughter.

A new husband and wife lived in their cottage. They had no children. One night the old woman heard noises coming from the garden and found the husband in her rampion patch. . .